Catch Me

Catch Me

the STEELE BROTHERS series
book 1

JENNIFER PROBST

Dedication

To Pat Chute, who is my mentor and my friend. You said I should quit my job and write more books. You were right all along - I'm having a hell of a ride. Thanks for everything you did for me and my family. And for anyone who has been afraid to leave…afraid to stay…afraid to be alone…you have the courage to make a change. Take the leap and people will be there to catch you.

Author's Note

I've loved writing the STEELE BROTHER series, and when I learned my rights were returned and decided to self-publish them with additional scenes, new covers, and a brand new installment, I was excited to share with my readers.

Please note these books are different from my other contemporary romance novels. The stories are erotic, with BDSM elements such as spanking, bondage, use of toys, and other explicit sexual scenes.

I never want my readers to feel disappointed, or misled, so if erotic BDSM is not your mug of tea, please do not read these books. I've decided NOT to use a pen name because my name is my brand, and I didn't want to confuse anyone. I also love writing every type of story, exploring different genres, lengths, and want to include these books under my own brand.

Thank you for listening, thank you for reading, and as always, thank you for your support. I hope you enjoy the story!

Prologue

*R*ICK STEELE TOOK IN THE CROWD at the Vesper Lounge. A bit light tonight, but he appreciated the elbow space. He ordered the famous Vesper martini and swept his gaze over the elegant, open space of the bar. Set in the Cosmopolitan Hotel, Rick enjoyed getting away from the chaos of the casinos. The excellent knowledge of cocktails from the staff only added to the appeal. The spill of pendant type chandeliers and waves of glass from the ceiling, generous bar, and brightly patterned comfortable seating let a person unwind from a hectic day. And God knows, he'd had a hell of a day.

"Hey, dude, I gotta present for you."

Rick turned at the familiar sound of his friend's voice. Dan was a bouncer at the casino and fondly dubbed the 'Brickhouse' from the famous seventies song. Rick put up a finger and a Cosmopolitan was slid in front of him a few minutes later. Rick learned the hard way not to tease his friend about his choice of foo foo drinks. He'd seen personally the black eye and broken tooth from the last chump.

"A vacation in the Virgin Islands?" Rick asked. "You shouldn't have."

"Better." Dan took a sip of his Cosmo, and slid an embossed black and gold card across the bar. The gold scrawl on the front read *FANTA C*.

Rick rolled his eyes, not bothering to pick it up. "Thanks anyway, but I'm burnt out on strip clubs."

Dan shook his head. "You're burnt out on everything lately, my friend. Look, I know you went through a bad time, but seriously dude, that was months ago. You gotta move on. You haven't had a date or a screw for far too long. Trust me, this'll be good for you. It's the answer to your prayers."

"Right. A strip club's going to solve all my problems. Go ahead. I'm listening. Really. I am."

Dan grinned, which looked more like a scowl from his meaty, gruff face. His brown eyes sparkled with excitement. "It's not a strip club, not even close. This is an *exclusive* club. Unlisted, of course, and the clientele are guaranteed privacy, discretion, and the night of his or her dreams."

Rick choked on his drink. The vodka burned down his throat, tearing at his eyes. "You're trying to hook me up with an escort service?" he questioned. "Seriously, I'm outta here."

Dan held up his hand. "You're not listening to me. It's not an escort service or has anything to do with hookers. Essentially, you give them your fantasy of who you want to spend one night with.

Your ultimate thrill. They match you up with someone who can fulfill the fantasy."

"Dude. No matter how you spin that, it's a hooker. "

"Not even close. The woman you're matched with have the exact same fantasies as you do. See, if they don't get a match, you don't get a call back, but that doesn't happen very often. Always someone out there who wants the same thing you do."

Rick frowned. "You're telling me they'll find me my perfect woman for one night? What happens after that?"

"You go your separate ways and no one says a word."

"Sounds like a hooker to me. A high priced one to boot."

Dan let out an impatient groan. "The fee is high, and you fill out a bunch of paperwork. It's a contract, but no one talks. It's just one awesome fuck. It goes no farther than that unless, of course, you both want it to."

"Then why is it called Fanta C?"

"Cause a lot of people *do* want sex and they want to experiment but they don't know how to go about it or find partners that will respect their privacy. You need to do something different, Rick. I'm worried about you and I think this will help."

Rick studied his friend, his features softening. It had been a long time since he'd played with a submissive, and hooking up in various clubs had stopped satisfying him a long time ago. He'd been craving a connection he couldn't seem to find in any of the normal or not so normal male/female hook up spots. Endless women and no one interested him beyond an initial conversation. Since he moved to Vegas, Rick had focused only on work, friends, and nothing sexual, much less intimate. Maybe Dan was right.

Maybe he needed to try something different.

Rick took the card. Turned it around in his fingers. A phone number was scrawled on the back in raised gold embossed numbers. "Is there a name I need to ask for?" he asked.

"No. Just tell whoever answers the phone that I sent you. When you're done, burn the card."

A grin tugged at his mouth. Things were getting interesting and precisely at the right time. "This is legal, right? Because if it's not, I'll beat the shit out of you." Dan laughed. "I don't play that way. It's totally legit. Just extremely exclusive. You won't regret it, Rick. I sure didn't."

Rick tucked the card in his pocket and nodded. They turned the conversation to neutral chitchat, but the seed had been planted, and all he could think of was the number on the card. And what it promised.

Maybe it was time to experience a new adventure. He trusted Dan. And maybe having one night to remember would kick start him out of his rut and his current sexual starvation.

He'd make the call.

Chapter One

*T*WO WEEKS LATER, RICK WONDERED if he'd made a mistake in making that call.

He tipped back his bottle of IPA and considered performing a Batman move and vanishing. The whole encounter seemed a bit too mysterious for him. When he dialed the number, he'd been connected immediately to an employee who seemed polished, nurturing, and thorough. He'd scanned back the contract and several intimate pages detailing everything he wanted in his encounter. Then he was promptly told if a match was found they'd contact him.

Rick got the call yesterday.

A name was sent to him, along with a short bio, and a meeting place. No further details.

He kind of wanted to kill Dan.

The new nightclub BLUE was the meeting place, and a main hot spot in Vegas, complete with laser blue lighting, pounding music, and a visual feast for the senses. The two level dance floor already held a rowdy group grinding away with some new dirty dancing and baring more flesh than glittery clothes. The music mixed with sprays of shooting water that occasionally drenched the crowd and brought up a roar of approval. His ears, which had long ago gone numb in Vegas, throbbed to the rhythm, reminding him he'd had a bitch of a day and made him wonder why he was here in the first place.

Rick bit back a groan and wondered again if he'd made a mistake. Dealing cards called to his soul, but a bunch of sore losers and drunks stomped out of the woodwork to torture him. He'd had to break up two fights, busted a card counter, and now he waited for a woman he'd never met in the trendiest club in Vegas, while he tried to ignore his blooming headache.

He curbed his impatience and took another sip of beer. Ever since he left Atlantic City for a change of scene, he'd been grateful. Vegas called to his sense of adventure and hard play. The past year proved he'd made the right decision, even though it was difficult leaving his brothers. A beautiful apartment, new job, and endless women stretched out before him in one glorious chorus line. He'd moved past his heartbreak and unleashed his single status on a number of very willing participants the first few months. Things were good.

Then why wasn't he happy?

He pushed the annoying thought away and tried to get a grip. OK, so Dan was right and it had been months since he last took a woman to bed. His choice. Hell, he'd thought Dan would applaud his selectiveness instead of urging him to accept a blind date through *FANTA C*.

Rick's lips twisted in mock humor as he set his empty bottle down on the trendy glass table. He wondered about the woman he was about to meet. Tara Denton. She'd obviously been through a brutal past and needed a tender hand. He was a natural Dominant, but used a gentle, firm touch. He was not into pain, and focused more on bondage for his submissive partners. After his encounters, though, he liked to keep his distance. Get in, and get out with his soul and heart intact. A little respect, a lot of pleasure, and no boundaries crossed. Of course, that's another reason he'd taken a break. Easier to wake up alone then face the empty feeling of meeting a woman's sleepy gaze and realize she'd never be *the one*. Or even the one for another evening.

Perhaps, Tara Denton was looking for the same type of thing. It would be so nice to enjoy a woman with no guilt, no expectations, and no letdown when the sun came up.

His phone vibrated. Muttering under his breath, he fished it out of his pocket and read the flashing text.

Tara Denton is in the Blue Lounge awaiting your arrival. Right corner table. Enjoy your evening.

His fingers paused on the keys. A slither of unease skated down his spine. His gut screamed once he agreed, his life would never be the same.

The screen went blank.

Rick shook his head to clear the strange fog and headed past the bar. The throbbing hip hop music dimmed as he made his way through a large tunnel of elaborate glass, displaying an impressive amount of golden statues in different forms of eroticism. He took a hard left, and entered the Blue room.

Aptly named, the quieter lounge area spilled an eerie blue light, reminding him of the Blue Grotto in Capri. The room shimmered from the floor to the ceiling with stunning crushed blue crystals embedded in every surface. A large aquarium tank took up one wall, displaying sea turtles, stingrays, and exotic fish in all sizes and colors. The sensual sounds of the flute and trickling water spilled from the background speakers, and gave the impression of another reality, just a few feet down from the main club. The exotic atmosphere impressed him every time he came into the themed room, even in Vegas.

He let his eyes adjust to the change of light and focused on the far right corner.

She sat with her legs crossed, neatly tucked under the glass table. A pink frothy drink rested in front of her, and she fiddled with the paper umbrella in nervous anticipation. She didn't look up, and Rick grabbed the moment to study her before she had the chance to put her guard up.

Her body was like nothing any tabloid magazine had tried to emulate with their extensive Photoshop and airbrush capabilities. This woman was the real deal. The plain photo that had been emailed to him didn't do her justice. Not even close.

He estimated Tara topped five foot, even with the three-inch heels she currently had wrapped around her sexy feet. She had obviously gone all out for their meeting, evident in the flashy silver top clinging to lush breasts, and the short black skirt she kept yanking down, revealing a good few inches of rounded thigh. She sported the perfect hourglass figure that pushed his lust buttons to an all time high, but never seemed fashionable for women nowadays.

Her hair was jammed up in a sophisticated chignon. Loose strawberry blonde strands popped out in an effort to be freed. She wore a bit too much makeup, but under the bright blue lights, Rick spotted the smattering of freckles and pure white skin that was a part of her Irish heritage. In a few seconds, he summed up one of her problems immediately. She was a gorgeous woman who didn't know it. She seemed uncomfortable in her flashy clothes, makeup, and heels. Rick bet she'd be ready to flee within minutes if he didn't walk over and close the deal.

He waited one beat. Two.

She looked up.

A foreign longing rose up and caught him in a chokehold. Aqua blue eyes widened as her gaze locked with his. The anxious worry he glimpsed deep in those depths caused a protectiveness to surge from within. His second thought centered on what she would look like when he thrust deep inside her and brought her to orgasm.

He hardened instantly. Son of a bitch. This was going to end up being an interesting night after all.

Rick held her gaze for a moment longer. Then strode over to the table.

Chapter Two

*T*ARA STIRRED HER COTTON CANDY DRINK for the fifth time and glanced at her watch. He was late, which meant he wasn't coming. A sense of relief surged through her. Thank God, now she could escape back to the sanctuary that was her room. It had sounded like a wonderful idea when her co-worker, Ginny, suggested Tara call the exclusive matchmaking agency. Ginny was one of the only people who knew about her relationship history, and her desire to get past her fears. Ginny urged Tara to sign the contract and be honest about what she wanted from her one night with a strange man. The expectations and limits were pre-defined, so Tara felt comfortable. Besides, Ginny had used *FANTA C* for a hook up and wanted to give her the referral.

It basically sounded like a dream come true. The perfect fantasy for twenty-four hours before she went back to reality. But sitting here in a trendy

Vegas bar, waiting for a man she intended to sleep with, was completely freaking her out. She didn't do things like this. Hell, she couldn't remember the last time she had on heels and make-up, let alone know how to flirt or go to bed with a man. She'd tried, though. No reason to blame herself. In moments, she'd rip off these hellish clothes and be in her comfy pj's under the covers. Alone.

Tara reached over to grab her purse, then did one last sweep of the room.

A man towered in the entrance, but his sheer height and width made her skip over him immediately.

Until he met her gaze head on.

Oh, God.

He looked like Thor.

Tara's eyes widened as she stared. He easily reached over six feet, with massive shoulders and muscled arms that seemed able to rip a tree out of the ground. He sported thick bleach-blond hair that tumbled slightly over his shoulders. His face was a contradiction of hard and soft with a sloped jaw, slashed cheekbones, and full luscious kissable lips. His green-gold eyes shimmered with heat and intensity. My God, what that man could probably do with a hammer. He gave off an energy that filtered through the room and hit her body with a jolt of electricity. There wasn't a female within miles that didn't bend to his unconscious male will. The group of sexy young women lounging by the bar had already taken notice as they stopped their conversation to give the man a once over, of course lingering a bit longer at his black leather pants. He topped off the look with a black t-shirt, which accented his power.

Her heart stopped. Then pounded against her chest in something close to a panic attack. It *was* him. But he'd looked so different in his picture. Less...intimidating? There was no way she'd be able to spend a night with him. He'd tear her apart.

Tara gripped the edge of the table. Breathe. She'd talk to him for a few minutes, explain she changed her mind, and walk away. Who cares if he was a literal walking sex on a stick? No way was she sleeping with someone more attractive than her. With her fat ass and scars, she needed someone to ease her into the experience, someone with gentleness and compassion. Not Thor, who'd burn up her panties in seconds and have her running in terror for the door.

He made his way across the room, in her direction.

Tara cleared her throat and forced herself to look calm. "Tara Denton?" His question was more of a command. She found she had no spit left when she opened her mouth to answer, and managed a squeak.

"Yes."

"Good. I'm Rick Steele." Those green eyes gentled as he pulled back the hip blue stool and took a seat. "Don't you like your drink? I'd be happy to get you another."

Tara looked down at her barely touched concoction and shook her head. "This is fine, thank you." She took a large sip and swallowed, as if to prove her point. The sweetness was a bit cloying on her tongue, but the vodka burned hot down her throat. Since she rarely drank, she fought a cough, determined to act cool. The slight curve of his lip told her she had failed.

He signaled the waiter over and ordered a beer. She forced her gaze upward, away from those large fingers inches from her own. Fingers that looked talented. The sudden image of those hands gripping her hips as he thrust inside of her caused her cheeks to heat. Tara took a deep breath and discreetly wiped her damp palms on her skirt. "Well, Mr. Steele—"

"Rick." Another quirk of amusement curved his lips. "I think we should at least be on a first name basis, don't you?"

His drawl reminded her of smoke, sex, and sweat. Tara nodded. "Oh, yes, of course. Rick. Well, I just wanted to let you know it will be perfectly acceptable if you'd like to cancel. I'm not sure if you saw my photo or read my requirements, but I understand if you decide to leave after our drinks."

He took a long pull of his beer, then pushed away from the table and studied her with interest. "You don't like me?"

Tara sputtered with embarrassment. "Um, no! I like you. I just don't think I'm the type you expected for a, for a…"

"One night stand?" he finished.

She nodded again. "Yes, that's right." She forced a smile. "Please don't feel bad. I appreciate you meeting me."

One brow shot up. "That's quite polite of you. But unnecessary." A wolfish grin transformed his face. A rush of sexual heat squeezed through her blood and settled between her thighs in an ache. "You see, Tara, I'm just counting the minutes until I get you into bed."

The breath whooshed out of her lungs. She blinked in confusion. Had she heard him correctly? No, he seemed to be staring at her with an open sort of...hunger. Nerves and arousal mingled and fought for dominance. She took another gulp of her drink, and then looked him squarely in the eye.

"Why?"

He laughed. The sound raked across her ears in a caress, the husky notes causing a low throb. Her body revved up like a racecar ready to shoot from the starting gate. She'd specifically requested a gentle, unassuming man who could slowly introduce her body again to the art of lovemaking. How long had it been since she'd desired a man? Most of the time, Tara needed to force herself out of the bodily deep freeze with her vibrator. Men usually caused a subconscious fear to drain away any lingering passion.

But not Rick Steele.

Hell, he'd probably command her body and soul if he got the chance. His dominant personality seeped from his aura, causing her panties to be wet with anticipation. But why on earth would this type of man ever be attracted to her?

She waited with curiosity for his response.

"I think the question is more like why wouldn't I. You have a body to die for, and in a matter of two minutes, you've made me laugh. Let's just say I'm dying to find out how many shades of blue your eyes will turn when I thrust between your thighs."

Hot color flooded her face. She shook her head. Maybe *FANTA C* hadn't told him her background. Damnit, she thought the man meeting her would know a bit about her past and what he faced. Tara gritted her teeth and made herself lift her chin in pride. "I'm sorry, but you must not have heard. I don't, I don't have a good body. Something happened to me and I have several deep scars that are quite... well... ugly. The man I met tonight was supposed to know that."

Those intense eyes of his turned ice cold. His voice lashed like a whip across tender flesh. "I know about your scars, Tara. I will not allow you to call them ugly again in my presence. Scars are the evidence of survival and life. Now, I'd suggest we continue with a much more pleasant conversation in my suite."

He dropped a few bills on the table, stood up, and offered his hand.

Seconds ticked by. Tara swallowed around the lump in her throat. Her gut screamed in warning, but the moment she touched his hand, she sensed she'd lose all control over this date, and be led down a path Frost would term the road less travelled.

Tara placed her hand in his and allowed him to lead her out.

Chapter Three

*T*HE DOOR SHUT BEHIND HIM.

Rick stepped back and let her gain her bearings. He'd booked a luxury suite for the evening, and the lush opulence stunned most newcomers. He watched with amusement as she tried not to let her eyes pop out of her head. Her gaze swept over the rich burgundy carpeting, expensive watercolors, and 14kt gold trim on the walls. The living area showcased a series of plush cream sofas with plump pillows, a large wet bar, and a private balcony that overlooked the entire skyline of Vegas. The tables were burnished mahogany and held endless vases of exotic blooms, their scent curling into the air in sensual abandon. Through the hallway, the bedroom beckoned. The oversized king bed made up of rich silvers and gold was set up so high Rick would need to lift her up. The image of her stretched naked on that bed teased him mercilessly. He imagined white skin and gorgeous strawberry blonde hair fanned out on the pillow, those blue eyes begging him to give her pleasure.

His opinion of *FANTA C* took a hard turn. Bored for months by an endless parade of women, Tara intrigued him within minutes of speaking. She was a mixture of prickle and heat, both shy and direct. Her discomfort about her body challenged him to change her mind.

Rick never backed down from a challenge.

Even now, those teeth reached for her lower lip and nibbled with worry. He watched the thoughts flicker over her face, obviously wondering if she'd gotten in over her head and how to get out of it. He tamped down a chuckle and made his way to the bar. "White wine?" he asked. "Pinot?"

She nodded gratefully, and he uncorked a fresh bottle and poured a glass. Her spiked heels sunk into the plush carpet as she took in the view from the balcony. Thousands of bright lights twinkled and flashed across the night sky, resembling exotic stars. The view of Vegas was nothing compared to Tara Denton's ass.

The lush curves made his fingers itch to touch and stroke. Sink his teeth into the sensitive flesh and take a bite. His cock hardened and he battled for control as he brought her the glass of wine, wondering if she'd notice.

Apparently, she didn't think she was worth an erection because she never bothered to check. He'd take care of that problem also.

She sipped her wine. Then took a deep breath. He waited.

"What do we do now?"

Damn, she was cute. He loved her natural fluster and how she barreled right through her own barriers. The woman had great courage, especially if her past was accurate. He lowered his voice to a sexy murmur. "What do you want to do now?"

Tara stepped back. Then caught herself. "Umm, well, I guess we get undressed now, right? Would you mind dimming the lights? Or do you just want me to wait underneath the covers for you?"

Rick realized she wasn't joking. Raw anger took hold, but he made sure he didn't reveal the emotion on his face. God, how deep did her scars really go? This asshole had not only hurt her, but also taught her that sex was dirty. That sex for a woman was getting naked under the sheets while a man got his rocks off. That this beautiful woman didn't think she was worth all that sex could offer her mind, body and soul nearly broke him.

"Stay here a minute."

He turned on his heel and marched into the bedroom. Yanked open the closet, and took out one of his white shirts. Then returned to the living room.

"Tara, can I ask you to do a few things for me?" He spoke with a tender tone. She nodded hesitantly. He reached out and touched her hair, still strangled in the tight bun. "Would you take your hair down for me?" He caressed her cheek. "Take off your make-up?" Then handed her the shirt. "And put this on?"

She stared at the fabric. "Why?"

He smiled at her confusion. "Because I want to see you underneath all of this stuff. And I want you comfortable."

He waited patiently while she seemed to digest his request. "Now?" she asked.

"Yes, please."

Tara nodded and walked to the bathroom. In a matter of minutes, she came out and stood in front of him. "Better?" she asked.

His heart stopped.

She was fucking gorgeous.

Heavy waves of strawberry blonde strands fell over her shoulders and tumbled in abandon. Her natural skin glowed, freshly scrubbed of all make-up, and showed off a generous smattering of freckles across her nose. Creamy white and smooth, he resisted the urge to taste her with his tongue and see if her flavor was as sweet. Her lips were pale pink and held a plump curve. But her body...

His shirt barely held in those lush breasts, even though she'd left on her bra. The hem fell right above her knees, and showed off muscled legs and pretty cotton candy painted toes.

"Oh, yeah, much better," he growled. "Turn around?"

Her cheeks colored, but she turned slowly in a circle in an attempt to please him. Her natural manner to give struck him. She obviously liked to bestow pleasure, and probably had that gift exploited to such a manner she was now afraid, but did it anyway. As she pivoted, he saw the line of her purple colored panties show through the shirt, the full globes of her ass begging for his fingers. But not yet. He needed to relax her first.

"Do you know how beautiful you are?" he demanded.

Disbelief flickered in those blue eyes. "Thank you, but—"

He closed the distance between them. She gasped as he grabbed her hand and laid it on his straining erection. "This is what you do to me. From the moment I laid eyes on you, I wanted you. By the end of the night, you're going to believe it, sweetheart. Make no mistake."

Her entire body shuddered, and power surged through him. He wanted to make her scream with pleasure, to cry his name as she orgasmed; until she couldn't remember the last time another man ever laid a hand on her. Possessiveness was not a natural part of him, but Rick didn't fight the urge. Instead, he embraced the basic male tendency to hunt. Conquer. Claim.

Her soft hand paused, and then gently stroked him. Rick groaned, and she seemed surprised that she had caused the pleasure. Bolder, she squeezed around the fabric of his pants and followed the ridge from base to tip. He held perfectly still and allowed her to explore. She took a step closer, until her breasts pressed against his chest. Immediately, her nipples hardened into perfect tight pebbles, and Rick fisted his hands to keep from touching her. Her arms came up to hold his shoulders, and her sweet breath rushed over his lips as she arched up on her tiptoes.

Then pressed her lips to his.

The tentative kiss rocked his world. Her lips were soft and sweet. He allowed her to explore the line of his mouth, gaining confidence, until the tip of her tongue slowly pushed into his mouth. With a low growl, he opened his mouth for her, desperately trying to hold back his instinct to throw her on the bed and spread her thighs. Her tongue swept in, thrust against his in a teasing battle.

Rick reached out and lifted her up against him. She made a little mewling noise, but he swallowed it as he claimed her mouth the way he craved. He drank deep, drowning in her taste as the scent of strawberries and flowers swam in his head. Within seconds, her body slumped against his and she surrendered, letting him drink his fill as her fingers thrust into his hair and held his head still for her own demands. Slowly, he eased back and looked down at her face.

Her lips were swollen and wet. Aqua eyes held a dazed sheen as she stared back at him. "Oh, my," she whispered. "That was so...good."

He laughed at her open response. "Believe me now? I want to throw you on that bed and get you naked. Touch and taste every part of your body. Then make you come so hard the only thing you can scream is my name. Get it?"

She nodded, obviously not able to speak.

"But I don't want to scare you. You specifically requested a man who's gentle and non threatening. I have dominant tendencies, but I would never hurt you, Tara. In fact, I'd tear apart the motherfucker who wrecked you for sex and caused you pain."

He watched her face carefully. There. The glimmer of arousal and need. Tara definitely had submissive tendencies, which he enjoyed in the bedroom. She obviously responded to a commanding attitude, but had been seriously scared off those types of men. He didn't blame her. But he intended to show her what she'd been missing with the right partner.

And he had all night.

"I'm asking you to trust me. Let go of your body and your control, and let me take care of you. I want to show you everything you've been missing. And the moment you tell me to stop, I swear to God I'll take my hands off you. Stop is the word when you panic, Tara. Ok?"

Seconds passed. She chewed on her lip. Indecision flickered over her face, along with a deep need to follow the tempting path before her. Rick waited with all the patience and calm in the world, knowing she had to trust her gut.

"Yes."

Excitement shimmered in blue depths. Triumph surged through him. He took her hand and led her into the bedroom.

Chapter Four

*T*ARA STOPPED BEFORE THE huge bed and swallowed back her instinct to yell *STOP* right now. Her senses were on overload with the most intense visual and physical pleasures. The luxurious suite closed around her with a pull to follow her baser urges. The huge mirror mounted on the ceiling both fascinated and terrified her. Her body hummed as Rick's fingers intertwined with hers in a firm grip she couldn't break, but she didn't want to either. Sweat broke over her as she fought the memory of another time, when she had given her trust and found everything turned against her. But for some reason, she trusted Rick. There was a core of gentleness within his control that spoke to her and promised no pain. Since she had signed up for this one night experience, Tara would push herself to the limit. She needed healing, and maybe the man holding her hand was the one to finally give it to her.

"Lie on the bed, sweetheart."

Humiliation washed over her. He'd look at her under the bright lights. His body was perfect and hers was completely damaged. Could she do this in front of a practical stranger? He sensed her nervousness and dropped a soft kiss on her lips. His voice raked across her ears in a low, hypnotic tone. "Turn off your thoughts and do what I say. I'll dim the lights."

Tara swallowed. She obediently and willingly climbed onto the high platform bed, laying her head on one of the stuffed pillows. She tugged the hem of the shirt down as far as it would stretch and waited for his next command.

Amusement gleamed in those tawny green-gold eyes. "You look like you're awaiting an execution rather than hours of sweet passion and orgasms."

"I'm so sorry," she said miserably. "I told you I'm not good at this."

"No more speaking. The only word I'll listen to from now on is stop."

As if on cue, a rush of heat sizzled down to her pussy. The sexiness of him being in charge of her caused her nipples to strain against the cotton of her bra. He nodded, pleased, as he watched her body's reaction. Then stripped.

The black shirt slid down his arms and hit the floor. His bare chest was carved and covered with golden brown hair. A thin line snaked down his tight abdomen and disappeared into the waistband of his pants. She didn't have long to wait. Rick snapped open the button and shed the pants, kicking them off to the side. He stood in a pair of black underwear that did nothing to hide the impressive erection in front of her. Instead of fear, Tara bit back a moan at the idea of having that whole length tight inside of her, thrusting, giving pleasure. A vibrator just couldn't compare to the experience of a man's flesh, and it had been so long...

His thumbs hooked into his underwear. He paused one moment to gaze directly into her eyes. Then revealed himself and all of his naked glory.

Tara sucked in her breath. Sheer, raw power beat from him in waves. He stalked over to the bed and let her drink her fill. His wolfish grin told her he liked her gaze on him, and a drop of liquid essence gleamed from the silky tip.

The idea she was the woman to cause such a reaction struck her hard and deep. She gripped the silk fabric of the sheets as she struggled to process the knowledge he desired her.

Rick placed one knee on the edge of the bed and leaned over her. She caught the scent of soap, musk, and man. Blonde strands framed his face as he bent forward, framing the hard lines of his cheeks and jaw. Those carved lips paused an inch from hers.

"Now it's your turn."

He began unbuttoning the shirt. Tara closed her eyes, dreading the moment of truth when he saw her naked, exposed. How often had her boyfriend called her ugly and maimed? Not worthy of his sexual attention?

"Look at me, Tara." Her eyes flew open at his commanding tone, snapping her back to the here and now. Fire shot from his eyes and burned into hers. "Gaze on me the whole time." She obeyed, helpless to break away. He undid each button with deliberate slowness, taking his time. Pushed the fabric down over her shoulders and off.

Her lacy matching lavender bra and panties was the only barrier between them. Pleasure shone in his face as he drank his fill, and then lingered on the scars.

Cigarette burns on her shoulders and the top of her breasts. A wicked knife cut across her ribs. Ugly gouged pockmarks at the top of her thighs. Tara imagined her reflection in the mirror as he looked at her, but she didn't hide from him.

After a while, he lifted his head. Her breath caught.

Hot, male desire gleamed from his eyes. His hard length pressed against her in demand. No revulsion, no shrinking away. Instead, he murmured low words of approval regarding her bravery, her beauty, how much he wanted her. His gentle, strong fingers caressed each nasty mark and it felt as though he could almost erase them away with his tender touch. Then with one quick action, he unclasped her bra. Removed the straps. And gazed at her nearly naked body.

"Fuck, you're gorgeous." His fingers traced the heavy curve of her breasts and lingered on the tight tips, begging for his touch. He followed one blemish across the right globe, and then lowered his head.

His tongue ran over her skin, wet and hot. Her body jumped like an electrical current, and she arched upward as he avoided her nipples and licked his way around her breasts. Sensitive and swollen, sensations raked over her and took merciless hold. A whimper escaped her lips as he palmed and plumped both breasts as a gift for his mouth. His breath whispered over her nipples and shot straight to her pussy. Then his lips closed around one tight bud.

"Rick!"

His name rang out in the room. The delicious sensation of her nipple rolled around between soft lips, wet tongue and sharp teeth all came together in a mingle of delight. He murmured encouragement as her mind fogged and refused to work, giving herself up to the demands of her body. Finally, he lifted his head and looked down. Her nipples stood out, erect and begging for more.

"Beautiful," he whispered. "Look how responsive you are. How sensitive. Your body was meant for a man's hands. I can't wait to taste your sweet pussy and see if you taste like strawberries."

Her pussy clenched in immediate response. He laughed low. "Rick?"

"No talking, Tara. The only word you need to remember is stop."

He pinched her nipple lightly. Hot currents sizzled down to settle between her thighs. Still rubbing her nipples with his thumbs, his mouth moved downward to kiss her belly. Dip into her belly button. Nibble teasingly along the line of her panties, pulling at the edge of the elastic with his teeth. Each time the fabric snapped back, she tightened with anticipation, but he ignored her unconscious pleas and busied himself elsewhere.

He pressed a kiss to the nasty wound on her inner thigh. His tongue sampled the crease between her hip and thigh, while his hands moved from her breasts to cup the firm globes of her ass. Through the barrier of fabric, he settled his open mouth on the core. Took a deep breath. And blew.

Tara shot up and cried his name. His moist breath teased her pounding clit. Liquid warmth shot out of her pussy. He pushed her back on the bed and took the top of her panties between his teeth. And inch-by-inch, he pulled them down.

Cool air hit her exposed folds. The intense contrast of hot and cold wracked her body with pleasure. Oh, God, when was the last time a man had his mouth on her? The vulnerability of her position suddenly struck her, and she realized he had her fully under his control. Her body stiffened as her mind flashed an array of images. Pain. Humiliation. Betrayal.

"Tara."

The sound of his voice lulled her away from the memory. His command brooked no argument as he looked up from between her spread thighs.

"Eyes on me."

His gaze told her not to think. Dominated every part of her soul, until she couldn't fight him, and she slipped firmly back into the present. Then he lowered his head.

His wet tongue parted her swollen folds and dived in. Her pussy clenched and throbbed under him, as he licked around her clit and tasted her juices. His thumbs parted her wider, exposing her, and she slid into surrender, glorying at her erotic abandon. The mirror on the ceiling showed her pink pussy lips spread wide, while his tongue took control. Her clit swelled and pushed from its hood in lusty demand.

Tara cried out and twisted against the bed, drowning in the pleasure of watching him command her body and push her toward orgasm. So close, she reached hard and desperately, but release eluded her.

"Please!" she screamed. She shook hard, panting, as his tongue traced circles around her clit and his fingers rubbed and stroked. The exquisite tension tightened every muscle in her body until she thought she'd die of the delight.

"Tell me what you want me to do, sweetheart. Tell me."

"Help me! Please help me...."

"Here you go, baby." His mouth sucked hard on her clit as his fingers plunged inside of her.

She came hard, screaming as convulsions shook her repeatedly. He milked her orgasm and drew it out, until Tara shattered as mini tremors took hold and thrashed her around the bed. The sheer intensity of such pleasure overwhelmed her. Spent, she collapsed helplessly underneath him, and suddenly tears ran down her cheeks.

He whispered her name and slid up her body. He kissed her tears away and held her tight against him. Tara felt cocooned in a secure warmth she never experienced; a promise of shelter from pain and heartbreak. Who was this man? How had he snuck past her barrier she erected in order to protect her heart and soul?

"Thank you." She snuggled closer as his legs entwined hers. His steady heartbeat thundered against her ear. A low chuckle stirred in her hair.

"Sweetheart, you have no clue how much pleasure that gave me. Thank you for trusting me to take you there."

The sudden realization he hadn't come made her body stiffen. Oh God, she hadn't gotten him off. Guilt assuaged her, and she broke his comforting grip, flipping herself over. The gorgeous lines of perfect carved chest muscles greeted her, and she dipped her head, kissing her way down. His breath hissed through his teeth in surprise as she tried to make up for her selfishness. She ran her hands down his thighs and gripped him between her palms.

"Christ, Tara." She ignored his plea, opened her mouth, and took him deep inside. His musky taste assaulted her senses. What had begun as a job turned to pleasure and desire for more, as her tongue swirled around the tip and she sucked him deep into the wet cavern of her mouth.

He let out a curse, and then dragged her back up. Every muscle stiffened as he forced her to settle against him. His ragged breathing cut through the air. Disappointment squeezed her heart. She hadn't done it right. He'd looked pleased, but her ex had consistently told her he'd gotten better blowjobs from a doll than her.

"Damnit to hell, stop thinking!" She jerked back. He lowered his voice and spoke through gritted teeth. "You almost made me come with the first lick of your tongue. But that's not what I'm looking for. I'm not ready to come until I'm deep inside you, making you mine. Understand? Now get that dickwad out of your head and come back to me."

Her mouth hinged open like a guppy. How did he know what she thought? How did he know her so well, after just a few short hours? And why in the world would he want her to be his?

The need beckoned and tempted like the slickness of Satan. To belong completely to a man again without fear. To give of herself without worry of being hurt. What a gift.

But one she promised herself she'd never receive again.

The truth struck hard. No matter how much pleasure Rick Steele gave her, no matter how well he read her thoughts, she'd disappear in the morning. She would never belong to another man again. Only herself. Tonight was about breaking down her walls and fear of sex. She refused to spend the rest of her life cowering from a man's touch. Rick had already shown her the best orgasm of her life. By dawn, hopefully she'd be more whole, and able to walk away with a full body and heart.

Alone.

Rick kissed her. His tongue swept in and took over, possessing every hidden nook and cranny until she dug her nails into his muscled shoulders and hung on. When he finally lifted his head, his eyes burned with demand.

"Sex isn't about tit for tat. Next time you take my cock in your mouth, make sure it's because you're dying to taste me. Not because you owe me an orgasm. Got it?"

His sexy directness re-ignited the ache between her legs. Her voice came out breathy as she forced the word past her lips. "Yes."

"Do you want more?"

Her pussy throbbed. Her nipples rose and tightened even further, His hand flicked the tip and she shuddered.

"I'll take that as a yes. Let's just make sure." His fingers slid down and plunged into her tight heat. Tara bucked under the sizzle of fire that tore through her center. Rick laughed. "Oh, yeah, that's the spot." He added another finger as he worked his way in and out, setting a teasing rhythm. Her already over stimulated clit throbbed and burned from the attention. In seconds, she neared orgasm again, completely swept up in the bodily demands he rang from her with his voice, tongue, and fingers.

He reared up and sheathed himself with a condom. Grabbed her ankles and thrust her legs wide apart. Again, her gaze snuck up to the mirror. Her pussy lay open and vulnerable to his every whim, and looking at their reflection made a sound of lust break from her lips. His huge, throbbing length lay right at her entrance, poised to push forward. She wanted him, ached, and then—

The memory surfaced. Expression twisted with rage as he pushed himself inside of her without thought, without care, hurting her tender flesh until...

"No, stop!" The words broke from her throat and she panted, trying to push the ugliness away.

"Look at me, Tara. Now."

She turned her gaze from the mirror to him. Golden eyes glittered and burned with heat. His hands gripped her ankles, but his touch was gentle. He kept perfectly still as he waited for her to calm and direct him.

"I would never hurt you. Say it."

"You will never hurt me."

"That's right baby. Do you still want me to stop?"

She relaxed; inch-by-inch, realizing she was safe. No, she already knew Rick would never hurt her. He wanted to give her pleasure. The last of the memory leaked away and left her body open, empty, needing him to fill her.

"No, more. I want more."

His hands stroked her inner thighs. His cock pushed one inch into her pussy, then stopped. Tara moaned, past the fear, only craving the bliss he offered. Another inch. The tip buried into wet, clinging heat. Her channel clenched and begged for more. One more inch. Another. Then...

"Ahhhhh!" She cried out as he plunged to the hilt, and then stopped. His massive length and width filled up every crevice, until there was nothing else left but him. Tara clung to his shoulders, digging her nails into solid muscle as she struggled with the invasion. The breath whooshed out of her lungs.

"OK?" he asked between gritted teeth. "God, Tara, you feel like heaven."

"Yes." She lifted her hips upward. "More."

"Here we go, baby. Hold on tight."

Rick pulled completely out, then surged back. The demanding pace drove every thought out of her mind but giving him everything he asked. Again and again, he drove deep inside and left nothing for her. Her body squeezed him with her dripping heat, and her clit pounded in demand. Each scrape against the sensitive flesh caused more shudders to spill through her. The tension tightened until every muscle in her body screamed for release. Still, he kept her right at the edge, not allowing her to fall over but demanded she surrender to each thrust until she had nothing left to hold back.

Something shattered deep within her and broke free. Tara arched and cried his name.

"Come for me, baby. Now!"

He pinched her clit and drove his cock inside one final time.

Tara shattered. Her pussy milked every inch of him as she convulsed, and then he followed her over with a hoarse shout, spilling his seed into her willing body.

No tears ran down her face this time. Tara succumbed to the delicious plunge into a cloak of warmth and safety, and finally surrendered to the darkness.

Chapter Five

*R*ICK SMOOTHED BACK THE STRANDS of strawberry-blonde hair from her face and watched her sleep. The physical and emotional release pushed her right into slumber, and he enjoyed the soft expression on her face when her mind shut off and there were no more barriers.

In a few short hours, Tara Denton had wrecked his world.

He'd never been with a woman who gave him such an honest, open surrender. Sure, he liked to play, and enjoyed dom/sub fun in the bedroom with willing partners. But he'd never felt so connected to another woman through physical intimacy. Not since Rebecca.

Her name skittered across his memory but without the usual sharp pang. Her deceit cost him big time. He'd stopped trusting and believing his partners, even in the bedroom, and that was a dangerous combination. Trust was implicit in a good relationship, and he used to pride himself on his ability to sniff out a liar a mile away. He lost his confidence in his own abilities, just like Tara lost her trust. A wry grin crossed his lips. They made quite a pair.

His gaze took in the scars that marked her body. Rage simmered, but he clobbered it back, knowing the emotion useless. Amazing how she imagined her body to be ugly. Tara awed him with her strength. She endured, fought back, and survived. Each wound was a testament to her soul, and he appreciated every damn one, like a soldier overseas battling in a war.

Her eyes flew open.

Rick watched her thoughts flicker across her face, then realize where she was. And with who. He enjoyed the slight flush to her cheeks and the easy way she blushed, which was a total contradiction from her open response in the bedroom. The way she begged his name and screamed as she came made him rigid all over again.

"Hungry?" he asked.

Tara sat up, propped on the pillows, and peered at the plates of food on the bed. "Starved? Are we having a picnic?"

He smeared some creamy goat cheese on a cracker and fed it to her. She moaned at the taste, and right then, he was rock hard and ready to rock and roll. "Just building up your energy for the rest of the night."

The flicker in her liquid blue eyes confirmed she was aroused at the idea of more play. He grinned and handed her a chilled glass of Pinot Grigio. "So,

Tara Denton, why don't you tell me about yourself?"

She gave a hearty laugh. The pleasant sound caressed his ears with delight. "You probably read everything in the report I gave to *FANTA C*. There's not much else to tell."

The dry facts of her brief bio barely scratched the surface. At least, with Tara. "Oh, I don't know. The report didn't tell me how much you liked me to suck on your clit before thrusting my fingers inside you. It didn't tell me your eyes are a thousand shades of blue and reveal every emotion, or that your breasts spill so perfectly in my hands."

She blushed. "OK, you win. What do you want to know?"

Evidently, she guarded her secrets well. "What do you do for work?"

Her muscles relaxed and she nibbled on some salted almonds. "I work for the local battered women's shelter part-time. They don't have the funds to pay very well, so I supplemented with a bookkeeping job at Mercier & Associates. I'm also working on my degree in accounting."

The pride in her voice warmed his heart. "I bet you're very good with numbers," he said slowly. "Numbers you can control. If you work hard enough, everything fits into place, with no surprises."

Her eyes widened. *Bingo.* His little accountant needed a place in her life where she felt empowered. Rick bet she'd squeeze out every dime of profit for Mercier.

"You're right. I never thought about it like that," she murmured. "After I fled, the shelter gave me career counseling. I was always really good in math and numbers." Her voice drifted off as if she fought the memory of her past, then she shook her head. Rick wrestled with his instinct to push. God, he wanted to know every thought and every hurdle she'd gone through.

"Did you graduate high school?" he asked gently.

Tara smiled. "Oh, yes, with honors. I loved school. I just never got to college because Tim wouldn't let me."

A dark cloud passed over him. "Tim? The one who hurt you?"

She seemed to struggle with her decision to share. Emotions shifted across her face, replaced with determination. Tara raised her gaze to his and looked him straight in the eye. "I don't like to talk about Tim much, but I'd like to tell you the story. If you want to hear it."

Rick gently caressed her soft hand, then squeezed. "Yes, baby. I do want to hear it."

She took a deep breath. "I met Tim senior year in high school. At first, he was the perfect boyfriend. Sweet, protective, caring. He took care of me. My father had taken off when I was young, and my mom wasn't really around." She crinkled her nose in distaste. "She had a series of boyfriends I liked to avoid, and I had no rules. No curfew, no need to show up at school. But I wanted to go to college, have a career, and be independent. I thought that's what Tim wanted too."

Rick waited patiently as she paused. "Things began to change. Tim got controlling. Angry. Hated my friends, and refused to let me talk to other boys. He said he needed me to concentrate on him. His father beat him, so Tim moved out and wanted me to live with him. I agreed, thinking I could go to the local community college and we'd support one another."

Tara swallowed. "I don't know when I realized he changed. Tim flew into rages over things I did. I started getting nervous all the time, trying to do everything right. The first time he hit me, I was so shocked, but he cried and swore he'd kill himself if I left."

Rick nodded with encouragement. He noticed she slipped into telling mode, her voice monotone. "I stayed. He began to beat me more often. My mother didn't want me anymore since she was shacked up with her new boyfriend. I had no money, and he controlled everything in my life. I kept missing classes from the bruises, so I dropped out of college."

"How long did you stay with him?"

"Three years. Two months. Five days."

"How did you get away, sweetheart?"

She shuddered. "I collected change. Loose dollar bills when I knew he'd been drinking. I stashed the money in one of the tile ceilings until I had enough. He always told me he'd kill me, then himself if I ever left. And I believed him. I had to be careful whom I involved myself with because I didn't want anyone else to get hurt.

"During the day, Tim worked at an auto shop. He kept a close eye on me and I wasn't allowed to leave the house when he worked his shift. But that day I did."

Tara closed her eyes. Rick wondered what horrors she watched behind her closed lids, and his gut wrenched. "I cut off all my hair. Put on a knit cap and Tim's clothes. Had a cab take me to the bus station. Then I bought a ticket to the next town. Then the next. And then the next."

His eyes widened. "You just kept traveling?"

She nodded."I travelled for two days straight to throw him off. Then I walked into the first church I saw and begged to be sent to the nearest women's shelter. This was back in California. I had a different name then, but I'm not that person any longer. Tara Denton would never stay with a man who raised his hand. She's successful and making her own way. And she'll never be caught again."

Her last words shot at him like cannon fire. Rick realized in that moment Tara had no plans to extend their relationship past tonight. This was no more than a healing ritual to free her body from her painful past. A strange panic coursed through him at the idea of letting her walk away. But her intentions had always been clear. Only his had changed.

Suddenly, Rick wanted much more than a one-night stand with Tara Denton.

"Do you live in Vegas now?" he asked carefully, stroking her silky golden red hair.

"Yes. I knew I'd have a new start here. Get lost. Find my own way." A glimmer of a smile ghosted her lips. "I like the idea of a tarnished city being my home. I can paint myself up with makeup, glitter, and clothes, but underneath, in the light of day, I always felt lacking. Tim used that to keep me a prisoner."

"But not anymore." Pride and admiration pulsed through his voice.

"Not ever again. Now I can give back. I stopped being afraid he'd find me. Therapy helped. But I still wonder...."

"Wonder what?"

She looked embarrassed, almost shy. "How a man like you could want me."

Her admission rocked him. "A man like me?"

"Yeah. Beautiful. Rick, there must have been a dozen women staring at you in the bar and wondering why you were taking me home."

Anger sizzled so hot he wanted to beat his chest like a caveman and howl at the moon in frustration. He never thought twice about how women viewed him, and just felt damn lucky when a female wanted him back. But evidently, Tara saw things differently. Her sense of feminine confidence had taken such a pounding; she didn't see what he did.

Words wouldn't help. Rarely did.

But actions would.

Rick studied her and wondered how hard he'd be able to push without causing her any painful memories. As a natural dominant lover, he decided to trust his gut, and watch her carefully. Lust speared right to his cock as he envisioned the scene laid out in his mind.

"Tara, did you like watching us in the mirror?"

The change of topic surprised her. She flushed, but he gave her credit. She didn't lie. "Yes."

He forced her chin up when she tried to bow her head. "Don't ever be afraid to say what you want or what turns you on. I loved how you snuck glances at the mirror and watched your body respond to mine. Do you know what my first thought was when I saw you sitting at the table?" She shook her head in obvious misery. "I couldn't wait to fuck you."

"Really?"

He smiled. "Really. I wanted to rip off that bra and suck on your nipples. I couldn't wait to see the look in your eyes when you came. And when you got up, all I could think of was getting my hands on your ass. In fact, I think that part of your anatomy has been sorely ignored tonight. Let's change that now."

Panic flared in those misty blue depths. "No."

He arched a brow. "Why not?"

"I have more scars on my back," she said softly.

"Then I'd say they need my loving attention." He plucked the wine glass from her fingers and put it on the bedside table, along with the plates of snacks. "Lie on your stomach, baby."

"No, Rick."

He gazed back at her with implacable demand. "Do you want to please me tonight, Tara?" She nodded. "Then I'm asking you to trust me."

Rick wouldn't have blamed her for refusing. Instead, after a few moments, she slowly turned around and lay down on the bed. Her hands cushioned her head. Her breath came out in ragged gasps as she fought the sheer vulnerability of being naked with her secrets exposed to his gaze. A deep joy and satisfaction clenched his gut as he gazed at the woman before him. Tara's pleasure came from pleasing her mate, no matter how scared she was. Rick swore she'd never regret giving him this chance to show her how precious she was. Her gift to him was priceless.

Rick took in the brutal marks that scattered her back and ass. "What are these, sweetheart?" He pointed to the perfect circle burns marring her upper back.

"Cigarettes."

"And these?" His fingers lightly traced the line of her spine and settled on the permanent welts on her buttocks.

"A whip. Sometimes a belt."

He winced at the thought of the blood and pain she endured under the bastard's hands, but made his assessment as quickly and clinically as possible. It surprised him that her marks made him want her more, to replace the horror with memories of pleasure.

"He was a bastard, Tara. But no one will ever hurt you again. Close your eyes and relax. Enjoy my touch."

He moved his hands to her shoulders and began a slow massage. The clenched muscles under his fingers refused to yield, but after a few minutes, her body loosened. Her breath evened out, and he knew immediately when she relaxed and let go. He spent a long time working her shoulders and upper back, enjoying the firm, white flesh, and couldn't help slipping to the side to caress the heavy globes of her breasts. She uttered a low moan and arched upward to give him access. He slid his hands underneath and gently plucked at her nipples, circling his thumbs around the rigid peaks. With a final pinch, he returned to his main task.

He worked the indents along her spine and watched goose bumps pepper her flesh. When her body was completely under his control, he concentrated on the swell of her buttocks. He massaged the lush curves and kneed her legs apart, squeezing her inner thighs as he continued without pause.

Her musky scent greeted his nostrils. Rick grinned at the swollen pink flesh, her juices gleaming in the light. Damn, she was a responsive little thing. His cock grew to full length and pulsed with demand.

"You're already wet for me, baby. Since you can't see yourself, I'll tell you what I see. A beautiful pink pussy, just begging for my fingers or my tongue. Your clit is hard but not enough. We can do better than that."

She wiggled on the bed and Rick laughed low at her reaction to the verbal play."But I really wish you could see this gorgeous ass of yours. All flushed and trembling. Arched high in the air, ready for my cock. But we have a long way to go."

He separated her firm ass and blew his hot breath on the sensitive rosette between her cheeks. Tara bucked, but he held her down with a gentle firmness that told her she had nowhere to run. He lowered his mouth and ran his tongue down the line of her ass, nibbling on the high curves as her arousal and the scent of strawberries mixed in the air. He opened her up wide and slid his fingers across her slit. She soaked his fingers, and he murmured in satisfaction.

Rick settled his mouth over the plump curve of her right cheek. Then sunk his teeth into the quivering flesh as he plunged two fingers into her channel.

She bucked and screamed. The orgasm took her hard and by surprise, and he rubbed her clit back and forth, forcing her climax to extend for long, long moments. His erection turned almost painful, and he quickly sheathed himself with a condom, rose up, and plunged his cock inside her wet, tight channel.

Rick massaged her ass, pinching gently, and then moved up to play with her breasts. She trembled, not able to see where his fingers would touch her next, and satisfaction ripped through him. He plunged in and out with a steady pace, deliberately rubbing her clit as it hardened and swelled again, poised for another orgasm.

"This is what you do to me, Tara," he said forcefully. "You're beautiful inside and out, scars and all. My cock loves your juicy pussy, all tight and welcoming."

"Please, Rick!"

He laughed as she arched her ass toward him, silently begging. "Not yet. You're not getting off again until I'm positive you believe me."

She sobbed as he pulled out of her clinging pussy and flipped her over with one quick movement. He pushed up her knees and spread her legs wide. "Look up," he commanded. Her dazed gaze rose to the mirror, the reflection of their naked, joined bodies in vivid detail. Her inner muscles immediately clenched, and Rick confirmed watching them aroused her.

He plumped her breasts and lowered his mouth to suck her nipples, tweaking the tips until they stood out, ruby red, and glistening. "This is all for me," he said, pointing to the mirror at her swollen peaks. Then he rose up and plunged deep inside of her.

Tara cried out. Her gaze helplessly glued to the mirror, she watched him pleasure her, varying short and hard thrusts until he found her g-spot. With a wicked grin, he pulled completely out and teased her clit with his finger, rubbing the bud in tight circles, repeatedly.

"I can't take anymore, please, Rick, oh, please."

"Your body is beautiful, Tara. Do you believe me now?"

"Yes!"

"Say it."

"My body is beautiful!"

He plunged directly to her g-spot.

"Ahhhhhh!" She screamed and came hard as her body convulsed around him. He kept up the pace and wrung every last ounce of liquid from her body, then let himself go.

His climax shattered him. The release started from his toes and shuddered out of his body, grabbing every inch and pumping it with heat. Her name broke from his lips, and then he tucked her tight into his chest and held her close.

Chapter Six

*T*HE FIRST WEAK RAY OF LIGHT struggled through the break in the blinds, reminding Tara that morning threatened. She pushed the thought away, and snuggled closer to her lover. Her body ached but she relished her sore muscles. She'd never been so delightfully used.

Rick Steele shattered every illusion she ever believed. Her limitations with sex. The fear of her body. The confidence in her sexuality.

And about being caught by another man.

Unease stirred her heart. She never felt more treasured or loved in her entire life, and realized Rick set the bar for all future men.

Tara wondered if she'd ever find another man in her life to match him.

"What are you thinking about?"

His low voice pulled her back into the moment. She smiled up at him, loving the golden arch of his brows, his glittering tawny eyes, the rough slope to his jaw. She traced the curve of his lower lip and he bit down on the pad of her finger, his tongue darting out to taste. Her breath caught as her pussy clenched. Rick laughed, as if he knew.

"I was wondering why on earth you'd ever need to book a one night stand." She caressed the stubble of his beard, loving the scratchiness against her flesh. "I'm sure women are begging you to take them on a daily basis."

He laughed again and pressed a quick kiss on her lips. "Thanks, sweetheart. What a nice complement."

"No, tell me. Why did you do this?"

The humor eased, and Tara caught a hint of vulnerability in his green eyes. "I haven't been with a woman in a long time."

Her mouth fell open like a guppy. "Get out."

A ghost of a smile settled on his lips. "No, truth. I haven't been with a woman for six months now. My choice."

Tara gazed at his naked chest. The man was sex on a stick and he'd been celibate for half a year? "Why?"

"I used to live in Atlantic City. That's where my family is from. I have three younger brothers, and we all followed in my father's footsteps and made our living as dealers in casinos. Anyway, first, my dad made us get a college degree, and then we were allowed to go to dealer school. In college, I met a girl Rebecca, and we pretty much were together the whole four years. On graduation day, I asked her to marry me."

Jealousy pierced Tara's heart. She resented the idea of another woman being pleasured by him. Claimed by him. She locked the messy emotion away and concentrated on his story. "What happened?"

"We began planning a wedding. Moved in together. Then I came home from work early one day and found her in bed with one of my groomsmen." He gave a humorless laugh. "Talk about a cliché all the way around, huh? At least he wasn't the best man."

Horror filled her eyes as she imagined the scene. The betrayal he must have struggled with. Already in one night, Tara realized this man gave his heart and soul without holding back. He'd demand the same of his partner.

A dozen apologies skittered through her mind to communicate. "Bitch," she muttered instead.

This time his laugh held genuine humor. "Yeah, that about says it. Needless to say, things got pretty ugly. After a few months, I realized I couldn't handle living there any longer. I needed a change. I decided Vegas was the perfect playground. I got a job quickly, settled in, and never looked back."

"That doesn't explain why you stopped having sex."

Rick shrugged. "When I first settled in Vegas, I went a bit crazy. Dated a lot and experimented with different women. Then my need fizzled out, and I only felt empty when I woke up in the morning. So, I took a break and concentrated on other stuff for a while. My hand has been my new best friend this past year."

He waggled his eyebrow in a bad Groucho Marx invitation. She giggled. "Sounds like my vibrator. It almost caught on fire these past few months and broke from overuse."

They laughed together. Tara stroked his chest, enjoying his crisp hair against her palm. "Do you still miss her?"

"No. Not anymore." Suddenly, his gaze locked on hers, glittering with a fierce intensity. "I miss this."

Joy broke through her at his words. But her heart pounded in confusion. What was he saying? Had he experienced the same strong connection she did? Did he want to continue when the night was over? Did she really want to continue?

Reality crashed around her. No. As much as she wanted more time with him, she had to stick to her plan. Work. Volunteer. College. She'd made herself a promise to never get involved with a man until she was whole. He'd given her a precious gift, but she couldn't risk pushing herself. She was still too fragile and suspected he might be too.

She just wasn't ready for anything other than a one-night stand. So, at dawn, though it would break her heart, she would leave Rick Steele behind.

Tara pushed away the strangled grief at the idea and climbed on top of him. Surprise lit his eyes as she straddled his hips, her hair falling around his face to wrap him in a curtain as she kissed him. She gave him everything he asked for in that kiss: her body, her surrender, her gratitude, and her desire.

Her tongue swept in and she greedily tasted his dark, male hunger. When she lifted her head, her gaze burned into his with promise.

"I'm doing this because I can't stand the idea of not having your cock in my mouth."

He tensed at her words. Then Tara slipped down his body, cupped his balls, and sunk her mouth over his hard, throbbing length.

Rick groaned. Cursed. She took her time, enjoying the taste of his salty flesh, licking to the tip, and then swirling around in teasing circles. His muscles clenched, and her nails dug into his hard thighs. Finally, she opened her mouth wide and sucked, rubbing and stroking the underside of his cock, scraping her finger nails over the sensitive flesh of his balls, while her name rang like music in her ears.

Suddenly, he stiffened and grabbed her shoulders. Tara knew he was about to explode, but she refused to move. His excitement blended and melded with hers, and her juices flowed as she rubbed herself against his leg like a cat in heat, sucking harder, harder, and then....

He exploded in her mouth. She swallowed him as he jerked helplessly under her touch, and then eased her mouth off his length. Sheer feminine power surged through her at his response, and in that moment, Tara finally slayed all her demons.

"What have you done to me?" he groaned.

Tara laughed, and then resumed licking him with gentle laps of her tongue. She stroked, rubbed, caressed. In minutes, his cock was hard again, stretched like iron encased in silk around her fist.

This time, he lifted her in one quick movement, and settled her on her hands and knees. A tearing sound echoed in the air.

"Rick, I, oh!"

His hard length plunged inside her wet heat. She moaned and pushed back into his hands as he rubbed her ass and pleasured her. Slow, delicious strokes filled her, driving her higher and higher. Her breasts hung down free, and he played with the heavy globes as he thrust in and out of her. The erotic abandon pumped through her body, tightening her muscles as she reached so close to orgasm. She circled her hips, searching for it, but he only laughed and kept his strokes shallow enough to tease but not get her off.

His hands pinched her nipples. Slid down her belly, and found the tight nub of her clit. He rubbed, using her juices to coat it, and then wrapped his fingers around her.

And squeezed.

Sharp pleasure grabbed, attacked, and threw her over. She cried out his name as every muscle clenched and released as ecstasy shot in waves over her. He came again, then collapsed on top of her in the bed, limbs entangled. Tara's heart beat as she breathed heavily, completely sated and praying for the light of dawn to never come.

***

His lips travelled over her soft skin. The heady scent of sex and strawberries hung heavily in the air. Rick stroked her lush breasts, her silky hair, and the curve of her buttocks. The red digits on the clock flashed with alarming rapidness.

He wasn't ready to let her go.

Rick closed his eyes and reached for courage. His one night-stand had become much more. He wanted the chance to date her. Cook her dinner. Make love to her in the daytime. Wash her in the shower.

Would she give him the opportunity?

Since Rebecca, he'd never had a soul connection to another woman like Tara. He also knew in his gut Tara was different. He knew now by experience, his ex-fiancée had always been selfish in her core. Tara held the soul of a giver, and a man would be safe giving her his trust.

So, he ripped down the last barriers of his heart and gave her the words.

"Stay with me."

Her body stiffened. She sat up. Her golden red curls tumbled wildly around her face. Aqua blue eyes held a mixture of emotions from his words. Fear. Hope. Joy. Resolve.

"What do you mean?" she asked. "We agreed to one night."

"Let's agree to more," he said. Rick reached over and took her hand. "Remember when we spoke about not getting caught? It's too late for me, Tara. I know it's crazy, that we've only been together one night. But you caught me. I want to see where this can lead. I want to see you again."

She flinched. Rick fought the uneasiness at her reaction and waited. It was time to push out of his comfort zone. This woman would walk away if he didn't try to fight for her. And by God, he would give it his all before he surrendered.

"I can't," she said softly.

His gaze dared her to speak the truth. "Why? You're attracted to me. We formed a connection last night. There's no reason not to take this further."

Suddenly, he knew. Her eyes filled with tears as she stared at him, all the naked emotion and vulnerability and fear on display. "I'm not ready, Rick. What you gave me tonight... the things you made me feel... I don't think another man will ever come close. But I made myself a promise. I'm not ready to commit to someone else yet. You gave me back my body, my mind, my freedom. You changed my life."

She closed her eyes and one tear leaked down her cheek. When she opened them, a hard resolve glimmered and shattered his heart. "But I'm not ready for a relationship. I need time to be on my own and find my own way."

Rick looked at the woman before him and realized he needed to let her go.

She was stronger than anyone he'd ever met. Sexy as hell, sweet as sugar, and not ready to give him everything. Emptiness poured into the spaces of his soul and threatened to stay. But damn, he needed to give her time to realize this was more than one night. She had already found her own path. She just needed to trust herself again.

Rick knew if he didn't leave now, he'd overpower her. Make her have so many orgasms she'd beg him to stay. Force her to accept they were meant to be together, and then she'd always wonder.

So, he shoved his needs and his wants into the depths of darkness, and locked it tight. Bent his head and kissed her. Her sweetness swam in his head and he breathed in her scent one last time.

Then rose from the bed and dressed.

"Thank you, Tara Denton," he said huskily as he paused at the door. "Thank you for giving me the best night of my life."

Rick opened the door and left.

Chapter Seven

THREE MONTHS LATER

*T*ARA ROLLED HER NECK IN CIRCLES and tried to ease the tension from her muscles. She groaned and closed the journal in front of her, pushing her calculator aside. Besides school and working more hours at Mercier, she had a serious case of tired eyes. It may be time to invest in some reading glasses, she thought, getting up from the chair and stretching her arms overhead.

Now, she'd be able to afford them. Satisfaction thrummed through her veins. Her work caught the eye of one of the partners, and she'd been offered a full-time job, including benefits. She switched to finishing her bachelor's degree online, which saved her commuting time, and gave her the opportunity to graduate faster. Everything she worked for finally clicked into place. She was finally happy. And almost complete.

Almost.

His face flickered in her vision, never far from her mind. Three months. She dreamed of him every night, and woke up with a fierce need that wracked her body. How many times had she picked up the phone to call him? How many times had she walked through the casino, hoping to catch a quick glimpse of him, knowing if she did, she'd never be able to walk away again?

Tara refused to do that to him. He was probably with a woman now. She pictured him kissing her, caressing her, giving her orgasms that shimmered with pleasure. Tara imagined his wicked laugh, the grin on his face as he touched her, the tender way he stroked her wounds.

Tara swallowed back the pain and straightened her back. It had been her decision. She had needed the time to realize she was strong enough to be on her own. Funny, she'd finally been convinced that giving herself to another man wouldn't change who she was. She'd grown up, grown strong, and stood on her own two feet. But now it was too late.

Too late to let him catch her.

She pushed away the sadness and opened the door.

"Hello, Tara."

She blinked and then gasped as the figment of her imagination walked into her office and stood before her. Immediately, her body softened and trembled, the intense waves of sexual energy whipping around her. God, he was gorgeous. She took in his figure with greed. Those long blonde locks tumbled over his brow, framing glittering green-gold eyes. He wore faded Levis that lovingly gripped his hips and thighs, and simple white t-shirt. His muscles strained against the fabric in an effort to be free. She remembered how he lifted her that night like she weighed nothing, sprawling her over his thighs as he plunged inside of her and...

Hot color flooded her cheeks. Satisfaction gleamed from his eyes, as if he knew her naughty thought. Tara clenched her fingers into a tight fist and fought for composure. "What are you doing here?" she asked.

"I wanted to congratulate you on your promotion. Working full-time now?"

Tara frowned. "How did you know?"

A smile touched his lips. "I know a few people at Mercier. I asked, and they said you've been doing very well."

She dug her nails into her palms to keep from reaching out and touching him. "Thank you. Yes, I'm very excited about it."

"Still in school?"

He paced the small office with deliberate steps, glancing around. She watched the tight swing of his ass as he moved. Then bit her lip, hard, to keep back a moan. "Ummm, yes. Taking classes online now which gives me more time."

"Sounds like a great plan. And the shelter?"

He grabbed a paper cup and filled it with water. Tara swallowed hard. She watched his gorgeous lips close around the edge as the cool liquid poured into his mouth and over his tongue. Heat coursed through her. "Huh? Oh, the shelter. I volunteer on weekends."

"That's good news. I'm glad you're doing well."

Irritation prickled her nerve endings. "Is that why you're here? To check up on me? Make sure I haven't fallen apart?"

"Nope. I knew you'd do fine. I was hoping you'd have dinner with me this week."

She blinked, confused. "Dinner?"

"Yes, it's not an odd concept. We get together over a meal and converse. Catch up."

"I know what dinner is. I just don't know why. I thought—I thought this was over."

His grin was all male and pure wickedness. "Do you want this to be over?"

No. Since she'd left, she'd grown stronger. She'd proved she didn't need a man to be happy, but God, she missed Rick Steele. Her heart pounded in growing excitement. Maybe it wasn't too late. "Why now?" she asked softly.

"You needed time," he said simply. "Time to know whatever you were feeling for me wouldn't threaten the life you choose to lead. I'm asking for a dinner date. Not to take over your routine or change things. Just to be with you. Will you let me, Tara?"

She studied his face. The warmth and determination in his eyes. The solidness of his frame. The patient energy swarming around him. He would never be like Tim, because he was a man strong enough to be gentle. Didn't she owe it to herself to explore something good and right for a change? It may have started with one night, but here he was, asking her to dinner. He'd waited three months, waiting until she was confident enough to accept the invitation.

"Yes. I'd love to go to dinner."

He nodded in an almost regal manner. "Excellent. Tomorrow night. Seven. I'll pick you up."

"Here." She ripped off a sticky note and scribbled her address down, pressing it into his warm palm. He grasped her fingers and lifted her hand to his lips. Then kissed her wrist, seeming to savor the rollicking beat of her heart.

"I'll see you tomorrow."

His words were a delicious promise and thinly veiled threat of what was to come.

Tara anticipated both.

***

Rick glanced at her from across the table, enjoying the view.

Her hand had trembled in nervousness when she opened the door, but she had dressed to please him. He knew she was conscious of her scars, but she'd worn a short black cocktail dress that hugged her lush curves and showed off the ripeness of her heavy breasts. Strawberry hair fell over her shoulders, brushing over that soft white skin. Three-inch open toe black stilettos made him fantasize of those heels digging into his ass as he fucked her. She was Eve incarnate, and all he wanted to do was take her in his arms and kiss her until she surrendered completely to him.

Instead, he'd smiled with pure pleasure, complimented her on the outfit, and led her into his black Mercedes.

He'd chosen a private booth in a small, intimate Italian restaurant that was known for their homemade pasta and sauce. Frank Sinatra crooned through the speakers, and the waiters spouted out lilting Italian interspersed between English. The tables were red, and white checkered, and candles burned brightly in the dim lighting. The setting inspired cozy conversations and spilling secrets.

He ordered a bottle of Chianti and some various appetizers for her to nibble on, then settled back in the booth. She flushed with pleasure at the attention. Tara deserved to be spoiled and treated like the vibrant, intelligent woman she was. Knowing she'd missed so much due to her abusive past made him want to beat the shit out of all the men before him. Instead, he reigned himself in, vowing to spoil her rotten and make her so damn happy, she'd never look back.

"I probably shouldn't eat so much," she confided. "I've gained weight these past few months."

His gaze narrowed in warning. "I like my women curvy and satisfied," he said. "I also don't like when you talk negatively about your body. Every inch of you is beautiful to me."

"That's how you make me feel," she whispered.

"Don't forget it."

"Then I guess I'll have bread."

He laughed and cut a thick slice, sliding the plate across the table. "See? You're a fast learner."

"You inspire me." She swirled the edge in olive oil, then nibbled at the crust. "Tell me more about your family. You said you have three brothers."

"Yes. I'm the oldest. Then we have Rome, Rafe, and Remington."

Humor glinted in her aqua eyes. "Oh, your Mama must be tough."

Rick grinned. "Hell, yes. We were all a bunch of hellions. She ruled with an iron fist, had eyes in the back of her head, and loved us so hard no one was afraid to mess with us. Dad retired finally, and they're living in Atlantic City, enjoying some well deserved time to relax."

"And you're all dealers?"

"Rome and Remington are. Rafe is in the military. I'm trying to get them to come out to Vegas."

She gave a sigh, her face full of longing. "It must've been so nice growing up with a big family. I'm an only child. Dad ran off when I was young, and I'm just not close to my mother."

He reached out and took her hand. "Did she know about how your ex treated you?"

Tara shook her head. "No. But she really didn't look hard at our relationship, or ask questions. She was a single mother, so Mom worked all the time. She played hard, too. There were many boyfriends in and out of the house. Some of them were nice, some of them weren't. I think that's why when Tim first hit me and wept for forgiveness, it wasn't as shocking as it should've been."

"Youth and first love is so fragile," he finally said. "I'm sorry you were hurt. But you not only survived, you thrived. You made your own way, Tara. That's very cool. Too many people out there wouldn't have the strength. They would've stayed."

Their gazes locked. Emotion shimmered around them, along with a leashed sexual energy that brought a low growl to his lips. Her pupils dilated, and Rick knew she was as turned on as he was. It was time to talk about other things in their relationship. Things he wanted to explore and dive into.

The waiter brought their food, added fresh Parmesan, and glided away.

"I want to fuck you."

Her fork clattered onto the plate. She winced at the sound, but her face reflected a growing arousal from his dirty talk. "Now? Here?"

A delighted grin broke across his face. "Would you allow me to?"

A frown creased her brow. "I don't know."

"An honest answer. Tara, I like to play on the sexual side of submission and domination. Do you know anything about it?"

"Yes." A shudder broke through her. "Tim liked to tie me up and beat me. I couldn't do that with you. I still have a long way to go, Rick. I get flashbacks, and nightmares. Not being able to move would scare me."

"I promise you one thing. I will never do anything to hurt you. I'm not looking for a contract or a safe word. I will never cause you physical pain unless you ask for it."

"Why would I ask for any pain?"

"Pleasure and pain is a fine line. If I bit your neck and the flash of pain took on immense pleasure, would you make me stop?"

Tara tilted her head in consideration. "No."

"That's the only type of pain I'd give you. I like to give commands that turn us both on. Everything I do would be for your pleasure. If you feel uncomfortable, or feel I'm pushing, you need to tell me. Communication is key between us. I want to know everything you're feeling and thinking."

"You make me feel like there's nowhere to hide anymore. It's a—strange feeling."

"Good or bad?"

"Both."

"Again, thank you for the honesty. Sweetheart, I don't want to scare you about expectations when we just started to date. But watching you across the table, nibbling on that bread, licking the oil off your lips, all I can think of is you on your knees with my cock buried in your mouth."

She sucked in a breath. Her fingers clenched around the fork, and the glassiness of her eyes gave him confirmation she liked talking about sex. About the things they'd do together. Maybe she'd like a bit of a naughty push.

"Would you like that, too?" he asked in a low voice.

"Yes." There was no hesitation in her breathy reply.

"Good. Now, before we dive into this delicious dinner, I'd like you to do something for me. I want you to go into the ladies room and remove your panties. Come back to the table and give them to me."

Her blue eyes held shock and raw lust. "What if someone sees?"

Rick raised a brow. "Take them off in a private stall. Your dress covers you properly. No one will know but me, and you."

Her pale pink lips parted. He shifted in his seat as his dick swelled so hard his jeans felt like they'd shrunk. He could tell she wanted to do it. He also knew she'd never done something like this before, so her brain was scrambling to recite all the logical reasons not to do it. Rick tested her to see her response.

His voice deepened with command. "I'm asking you to do this for me, Tara. Now."

One second. Two. Three.

She rose from the booth and clicked away on her high heels. He waited, picturing slipping off the lacy material down her legs. Imagined putting them in her tiny purse. Imagined how her pussy would soften and grow wet at the idea she was bare underneath the proper black dress.

Finally, her heels alerted him and she slid back into the booth. Her body was trembling like a fine tuned instrument. Her skin was a light rosy pink, and her pulse beat madly at the base of her throat.

Rick reached across the table, palm open. "Good girl. Now give me the panties."

He waited. She bit her lip, looked down at her purse, and hesitated. Slowly, she handed over a tiny scrap of black lace, closing his fingers quickly around the wad of material.

Discreetly, he tucked the panties in his pocket and looked at her. Lust glittered from her features. HIs smile was slow, and pure wicked. "Thanks sweetheart. Now, eat your dinner and enjoy. I know

I will. I'll imagine your pink pussy begging for my fingers. I'll imagine how later I'll tease your clit, push inside you, and make you come so hard you'll cry my name."

Then he began to eat.

Chapter Eight

*T*ARA WAS SLOWLY GOING out of her mind.

She was having a conversation in a public restaurant with no panties.

And she loved it.

She ate the delicious, homemade ravioli and sipped her wine. She listened to Rick's stories about growing up with his brothers, laughing at their antics, and enjoying the warmth in his eyes while he spoke. At the same time, she was excruciatingly aware of her body. Every inch of her skin burned. Her muscles tightened with the effort to keep herself from launching across the table to make him ease the ache inside. Her pussy leaked wetness down her thighs, and she kept shifting in the chair, trying to find some relief. Her breasts swelled, causing her nipples to tighten and press against the scratchy lace of her bra in agony.

Her senses went into high alert, almost like an animal venturing outside. The scent of Rick's musky cologne mixed with Italian herbs and sauce was utterly intoxicating. The coolness of leather beneath her sensitive ass cheeks only increased the desire. The languorous slide of red wine down her throat, warming her blood.

The man was a wizard. Throughout the meal, he'd lean over and slide his fingers over her arm, causing goose bumps to prickle her flesh. His leg pressed against her bare calf, and when the waiter came to ask if they needed anything else, he deliberately used his foot to kick her legs apart, freaking Tara out that the waiter could smell her arousal.

It was torture. It was decadent. It was heaven.

"Are we ready?" he finally asked.

Her legs trembled. She wondered if she'd be able to walk out of the restaurant on her own power. "Yes, please."

Tara managed to get up, and he gripped her elbow, guiding her out to the sidewalk. The muggy, hot air closed around them, adding to the sensuality of the evening. He opened her door, and minutes later; they pulled away and drove down the famous Vegas strip.

The flashing neon lights glittered and the moon hung in the sky like a ripe fruit. "Did you enjoy dinner?" he asked.

Tara bit down on her lower lip to stop from asking him to do all sorts of filthy, delicious things to her. "Yes."

"I'm glad. Sweetheart, lift up your skirt and prop both feet on the dashboard."

She gasped. Swung her gaze around. He kept his eyes on the road, only a slight smile giving away his amusement at her reaction. "People will see me! I can't do that."

"My windows are tinted. No one can see you. I will never embarrass you, Tara. I will never ask you to do something that may hurt your career, " he said seriously. "Our play is for pleasure only. Do you understand?"

Slowly, she nodded.

"Then please do as I ask. Keep the shoes on."

Practically dripping with her arousal from the demand, Tara began to soften and relax into a place where she didn't have to control her thoughts. An odd sense of freedom beat inside her. Freedom from everyone, and anyone's opinion. Freedom from her own constant mental chatter. More importantly, freedom from the endless responsibilities of daily life. Here, in the car with Rick, she only had to obey his commands.

Tara lifted her skirt. Then placed her feet on the dashboard.

"Wider. I want you to spread your legs so you're open to me. Lift your dress up to your hips. I want to be able to gaze at your beautiful pussy."

A low moan escaped her throat. She hiked the dress higher, and spread her legs wide. Her clit throbbed for pressure. Tara was sure just a light swipe of pressure would hurl into orgasm.

"Perfect. My God, you're so hot. So sweet. Do you still taste like vanilla ice cream?"

Her breath shuddered and her eyes half closed.

"Let's find out."

One hand reached across the seat. Lightly caressing her inner thighs, he ran a teasing finger upward, tracing her labia and deliberately ignoring her throbbing clit. He took his time, his thumb grazing the hard nub so lightly; she bit her lip to keep from crying out. Tara tried to stay still and not twist or arch for more, and almost as if he rewarded her, suddenly his fingers plunged inside, curling just enough to hit that delicious spot inside her.

She threw her head back and yelled his name. Those wicked fingers played her like a finely tuned instrument, stroking and teasing just right to drive her slowly out of her mind. Plunging in and out of her wet, clenching channel. Then he removed his hand.

Tara bit back a whimper. He lifted his fingers to his nose and breathed in her scent. She watched him with half fascination, half shock as he sucked on his fingers, licking her essence as if she were a tasty snack he enjoyed devouring. Her heavy breathing filled the car.

"Yes, perfect. Vanilla was always my favorite flavor."

"Rick—"

"I know. You want to come. But half the fun is playing the edge. I love watching you become aroused for me, until all you care about is getting me to fuck you. I want you to be crazy for me, Tara."

"I am. I've never felt like this before. Please."

He veered the car off the road, and parked. Tara realized they were back at her apartment. Shaking with pure need, she waited for his next command, her gaze fixed on his face.

Rick unbuckled his seat belt and reached over. Slowly tracing the curve of her lips, his features softened. "You're so fucking beautiful. Inside and out." He ducked his head and kissed her deep and hard, his tongue thrusting inside. She hung on to his shoulders, letting him take over her mouth and her body and her heart. Finally, he broke the kiss and gently smoothed her dress back down her legs to cover her.

Tara blinked in confusion. "Aren't you coming in?" she asked raggedly.

"No."She jerked with the rejection, but he tangled his fingers in her hair and forced her to meet his gaze. "Listen to me, sweetheart. I want you so bad I may explode in my pants like a damn teenager. But I just found you again and I want to move slowly. The next time you're in my bed, you're never leaving again." Those green-gold eyes glittered with lust and determination. "Next time you're in my bed, I want to know you're mine."

The truth shook through her. His patience and control allowed her to surrender, knowing he'd keep her safe. Knowing he'd care for not only her body, but also each emotional part buried deep inside.

If she was ready.

Tara shook with indecision. Her need for orgasm and to be held in his arms dominated her mind and her body. But she was afraid for her last wall to crumble and leave her vulnerable again.

He watched her and slowly nodded, accepting her hesitation. "Will you join me for dinner again tomorrow? I can show you my apartment. I'll cook."

Her body screamed for her to demand the orgasm promised. Every inch of her skin felt sensitized, like she was in a higher state. Rick was right. She wasn't ready, and she needed more time. "Yes."

He got out of the car, guiding her carefully over the crooked pavement, and walked her to the door. He kissed her again and waited until she got her key.

"Good night, Tara."

"Good night, Rick."

She closed the door, already looking forward to tomorrow.

Chapter Nine

*R*ICK FINISHED THE PREP on dinner and wondered if he should go jerk off before Tara arrived.

Cursing under his breath, he pushed back the need and swore he could handle it. Discipline and abstinence was good for a Dom, reminding him every move was done for her pleasure. He was playing for keeps, and he needed his gaze kept on the goal.

Still, chastity was a bitch.

His cock throbbed and wept to bury himself in Tara's sweet body. For the past three weeks, they'd fallen into a comforting routine that relationships were built on. They'd usually dine together; taking turns cooking depending on his shifts and her homework schedule. Sometimes, she visited him at the casino and tempted him with sly glances and tight skirts, walking past his table on fuck-me heels, until the draw of the cards was nothing compared to the draw of her lush breasts and swinging ass. Of course, her punishment had been worth it. On his break, he'd slipped her a bullet vibrator and commanded her to put it inside of her pussy and walk past him a minimum of ten times.

By the final turn, her face was flushed, her legs trembled, and Rick gauged she'd had two orgasms so far.

After work, he'd given her two more.

Her trust in him was implicit every time she obeyed his commands. The bond grew stronger each day, and Rick swore he wouldn't take her to bed until she was ready to give him everything.

The doorbell rang.

He padded on bare feet and opened it. "Hey." Her upturned face was wreathed in her usual open smile, and she kissed him with an honest passion that shook him to the core. He'd never met a woman like her. Face scrubbed of make-up, hair twisted in a high ponytail; she wrinkled her pert nose and stepped inside dressed in yoga pants and a tight t-shirt that strained across her chest.

Best. Outfit. Ever.

"I'm sorry I look like this," she said hurriedly. "I had to work late, and tomorrow is my midterm and I'm kind of freaking out. I don't know if I'll pass."

He grinned and tugged at her ponytail, shutting the door. "You always say that. Then you get an A."

"I mean it this time." She dropped a stack of folders on the coffee table and groaned. "I'm gonna fail."

Rick handed her a glass of Chardonnay. "Then you'll study until you feel like you'll get an A."

"This isn't fair to you. Your head's going to explode with statistical reasoning and audit principles."

"Piece of cake. I deal cards, remember? I'm a math whiz. First, let's eat for strength, and then get to it."

They feasted on chicken, green beans, and roasted potatoes. Rick watched her chattering away about her courses, her new client she'd inherited at Mercier, and the latest episode of Homeland. God, she'd changed. Her natural vibrancy and joy for life shone in the burn of her blue eyes, so very different from when he'd first met her. How had his entire life changed in a matter of a few months? It was as if all this time he'd been missing a piece of himself he never knew about until he walked into that club.

"Uh, oh. You're staring at me funny. I'm babbling again, aren't I?"

He laughed. "You babble beautifully."

"Then what's that look on your face?"

He lowered his voice to that commanding tone he knew got her hot and ready. "Just thinking of the ways I'm going to make you come tonight."

Her breath hissed from her teeth. "Oh."

Rick winked. "Yes. Oh is probably a good response. Now finish your chicken."

She did, but he could tell she was distracted from his last statement. Good. He liked her on edge, anticipating what was next. He now owned her orgasms. Her body already responded just to the deepening of his voice, or an implacable stare. Tara had natural submissive tendencies, a desire to please, and sweet freedom in obeying his commands. She was a strong woman who finally owned her sexuality and needs without that asshole haunting her.

They cleaned up together and she stood by the couch, awaiting his command.

His lips twitched in a wicked grin. "Time to hit the books. Where are we starting?"

Disappointment flickered on her face. Rick bet if he slipped his fingers under her stretchy pants, she'd be drenched. "We can study later," she suggested hopefully.

He shook his head and took a seat on the oatmeal colored sectional. "Nope. Work first. We want to make sure you get that A."

"I'm feeling more confident now."

"Tara." His voice held a clear warning. "Do you want to go home without an orgasm tonight?"

She let out a long sigh. "No. Okay. Work first." Her grumble was charming, and he hid another smile as he settled down.

"Why don't we go over the practice tests first?"

She sifted through papers and pulled out a green sheet with endless numbers on them. "I suck at these theory questions."

"We'll start there."

Rick settled in for a long night of studying.

***

Tara laid her head back on the soft couch and groaned. "No more. I can't. My eyes hurt."

"Are you getting an A?"

A shiver spread through her body at the growly command. God, when she spoke to her like that she melted into a gob of Jell-O. So. Hot. "Yes. I'm getting an A."

"Good girl."

Rick shut the folder and stretched out his long legs. She studied his body with pure appreciation. Even his bare feet were sexy. He wore casual sweat pants and a faded tank that showed off his bulging biceps and rock hard physique. His gorgeous caramel hair brushed his shoulders, framing his face, accenting sculpted lips with dark golden stubble hugging his jaw. He was a man who held an innate grace and leashed power that made people automatically step out of his way, and women to flock. Somehow, someway, he only wanted her. And he wanted her bad enough to wait for her to be sure, refusing to claim her until she made her decision.

The fragile wall protecting the last of her defenses shuddered and began to crumble. He spent his hours doing homework, making sure she would ace her tests. He cooked dinner, always escorted her to the door, held her hand, and told her she was beautiful every time he saw her. He gave her countless orgasms and never asked for himself. He was a man she could trust, believe in, and build a life with side by side, because he'd never try to make her into something or someone she wasn't.

And Tara was madly, irrevocably, completely in love with him.

As if he sensed her change in mood, he swung his head around and pinned her with his gaze. The air shifted, sizzled, and Tara knew nothing would ever be the same, and it was good. So very good.

"Do you want to tell me something, Tara?"

His voice was a whisper of seduction. A velvety, dark command. Green-gold eyes glittered with raw lust, possession, and pure love.

"I love you, Rick Steele. I have since the night we met, but I wasn't ready. But I am now. I want to give you the pleasure you give me. I want to give you my body, and my heart. You helped me see I'm beautiful, and worthy of love. You helped me see...everything."

"About damn time."

In one swift motion, he lifted her up from the couch and into his arms. His mouth claimed what was already his, tongue thrusting between her lips and gathering up her taste, while she clung to him, desperate to feel his body naked over hers.

"I love you, too. I wanted to give you time to realize you're strong enough to handle me, or any man. I want to know your favorite color and food, the shampoo you use, and what side of the bed you prefer to sleep on at night. I want to fuck you for hours and lose myself in your sweet body. I want to support you in every way, watch you graduate, and stand beside you while you fly. Then I'll be right there to welcome you back. Do you get it now?"

Oh, yeah, she got it. Rick Steele had given her a gift more priceless than diamonds. Time. She choked on a sob and he lifted her higher, carrying her into his bedroom. He lowered her back to the ground inch by inch, so his hard cock dragged over her sensitive pussy, her tummy, her nipples, until her toes touched the thick carpet.

"Strip," he commanded.

She took off her clothes with shaking hands, until she stood naked before him. With a needy moan, she lifted her hands to him, palms up, in a gesture of submission.

"Let me please you."

He stroked his cock, making her mouth water for the taste of him. "Ask for what you want, Tara."

"Please let me suck your cock."

"Good girl."

She dropped to her knees and lowered his pants. She hissed out a breath when she found him with no underwear, and his thick, hard cock sprung free, waiting for her. Tara lowered her head, opened her mouth wide, and took him in.

His fingers tangled in her head and he held her firmly as she sucked hard, her tongue swirling over the head while she massaged his balls, scraping her nails lightly against the sensitive flesh. Rick let out a litany of curse words, and she sucked harder, opening wider, until he hit the back of her throat and his hips jerked with the start of his release. Then his hot semen spilled down her throat, and her name ripped through the air like a prayer. She took it all, relishing her power and his need for her, slowly easing him out of her mouth when the last of his orgasm had dissipated.

"Thank you my beautiful girl. I love you. And if I don't get inside your sweet pussy right now, I'm going to die. Now, climb on the bed and get on all fours."

She did, spreading her legs wide so he could see how much she needed him. She heard the tear of a wrapper, and the bed dipped. His hands cupped her breasts, rubbing the tips, playing, and teasing until her nipples were hard, long, and so sensitive they bordered on pain. He rained kisses down her spine; licking her scars with loving attention, and eased his cock inside her dripping heat, inch by slow inch. She rocked back, moaning in need, wanting him to take her hard and fast, but he ignored her, swiping his dick over her labia, brushing her clit, then easing into her entryway again before stopping and repeating the whole movement again.

"Please. Oh, please."

"I intend to, sweetheart. Oh, I love your hot pussy. How bad do you want me to fuck you?"

"So bad! I'll do anything, please."

He pushed in another few inches. His thumb rotated a nice steady pressure on her clit. Everything inside Tara froze in anticipation of an explosive climax, hovering on the sharp edge. She shook with the excruciating agony of wanting him to push her over. He massaged her clit from the sides, his cock halfway there, her nipples begging for more pressure, and then—

"Come for me, Tara."

He surged inside with one hard thrust and pinched her clit.

Tara screamed, falling over the edge, her body convulsing in a release so exquisite she felt shattered and then put back together again. The orgasm went on and on, and he threw her into a second one by never slowing the pace, keeping pressure on her clit, and pinching her nipples. Finally, Tara collapsed on the bed, shaking, and crawled into his arms.

Tears leaked from her eyes and he held her, kissing her head, his hard hands stroking her body and letting her find the release. Her tears cleansed. Healed. And he never let her go, saying over and over she was precious and he loved her.

"Thank you for not giving up on me," she whispered.

"Thank you for letting me catch you."

He kissed her slow and gentle, and Tara knew her future was bright, and beautiful, and full of possibilities.

The End

Jennifer's Playlist

Everything Has Changed - Taylor Swift/Ed Sheeran

Ghost Town - Adam Lambert

Marvin Gaye - Charlie Puth

A Higher Place - Adam Levine

Lost Stars - Adam Levine

Run Run Run- Kelly Clarkson and John Legend

Lean On - MO & DJ Snake

All That I Am - Rob Thomas

Song for Someone - U2

Sugar - Maroon 5

About the Author

Jennifer Probst is the New York Times, USA Today, and Wall Street Journal bestselling author of both sexy and erotic contemporary romance. She was thrilled her novel, The Marriage Bargain, was the #6 Bestselling Book on Amazon for 2012. Her first children's book, Buffy and the Carrot, was co-written with her 12 year old niece, and her short story, "A Life Worth Living" chronicles the life of a shelter dog. She makes her home in New York with her sons, husband, two rescue dogs, and a house that never seems to be clean. She loves hearing from all readers! Stop by her website at http://www.jenniferprobst.com for all her upcoming releases, news and street team information.

Made in the USA
San Bernardino, CA
24 March 2016